Blissful Tales
of the ♥

The contents of this work, including, but not limited to, the accuracy of events, people, and places depicted; opinions expressed; permission to use previously published materials included; and any advice given or actions advocated are solely the responsibility of the author, who assumes all liability for said work and indemnifies the publisher against any claims stemming from publication of the work.

All Rights Reserved
Copyright © 2021 by Ricky Gallegos

No part of this book may be reproduced or transmitted, downloaded, distributed, reverse engineered, or stored in or introduced into any information storage and retrieval system, in any form or by any means, including photocopying and recording, whether electronic or mechanical, now known or hereinafter invented without permission in writing from the publisher.

Dorrance Publishing Co
585 Alpha Drive
Suite 103
Pittsburgh, PA 15238
Visit our website at www.dorrancebookstore.com

ISBN: 978-1-6470-2007-1
eISBN: 978-1-6461-0663-9

Blissful Tales
of the ♥

Ricky Gallegos

THIS BOOK IS INSPIRED BY
MY LOVELY AND BEAUTIFUL WIFE

Terri Gallegos

SHE HAS SHOWN ME
WHAT PURE AND TRUE LOVE IS.

Porcelain Doll

I see you through the glass case.
You seem to be speaking to me.
You wave me to come closer to the pane.
I touch the reflection of you as if i can caress your lips.
You smile at me and mouth (i miss you too)
Only if i could break this glass to have you come out of your tomb.
Stroking your hair back you nod in sheer disbelief.
As i try to shatter the glass.
As if my strong hands could free you.
No rock, no hammer can free you.
Although i have tried.
Biting my lip, i need to know how soft your blonde hair is.
I dream of that day i may be able to hold and hear you.
Just for a moment. Is all i pray for.
You look saddened as that thought passed through my mind.
It has been my visiting time.
Gently i put you back on your dome glass shelf.
Until i come back for you another time.
I will never leave you alone.

Playgrounds

◆

Walking into the drift.
You feel at home alongside the reefs.
As the bluegills swarm your toes.
Warm is the waters of yesterday.
As the sun sets on you.
You see the ever-changing blues and greens
and a hint of purple gleaming from the school of fish.
As if they were saying hello to you.
Do the bluegills follow your steps on the soft sands of tomorrow?
Above are the seagulls searching for food.
Like the scavengers of times past as it dissipates into yesteryear.
Diving into the tides with the fish is your playground.
The clean and warm waters of life wash you
from the grime of the nightmares.
Stay in the warm corals where you are safe from the land sharks,
That devour souls and dreams.
Swim from the riptides that seem dangerously fun.
For they will send you adrift into the piranhas that
nibble until there is nothing left.
Until the sun rises again, the sunfish will guide your paths well.
Stay by them.
For all eternity.
Until that starfish shines on you again.
For he is coming soon.

The Looking Glass

◆

the looking glass
as i stumble across your mirror
i peek into the past
toward what you have seen
within this glass
behind the glass is a void of black
to reflect your image
a thin haze of nothing
cannot be seen
transparent is the void
as if it does not exist
only to be seen by the creator
a red smudge
is visible on the glass
a mistake of a lipstick
to know this is yours
envisioning your look
as you prepare for the day
seeing as only a dream
the wet long blonde strands
dangling in front of your eyes
shirtless you are
staring intently at your breasts
you look puzzled

grimacing like you were going to ask a question
you wave your hair back behind your ears
knowing i am not even with you
i see the disapproval from your eyes
left speechless
i call to you
dear, my love
why are you unhappy
don't you know every woman is mad
about how you all see yourselves?
pointless to me
i feel for you, my sweet
it's not what you look like
nor is it the definitions of all your curves
that make you the perfect girl i see
look beyond this image of you before yourself
look beneath the skin
beneath the tissues
beneath the makeup
beneath the ribcage
it's right there
glowing bright and beautiful as you are
it is smudge free
it is your glimmering soul.

it is pure
it is flawless
incomparable and seen by the blind eye
it lays within you
unbroken
strong as a dragon
it is precious
priceless
cannot be held by the hand of man
cannot be seen by machine
but can be heard in your voice
as i stand and look into your glass
i understand all that you are
all that you want to be
i tell you
you do not need this glass
for you are pure of love
full of beauty
to even shatter this glass
would not reshape the
essence of you
of Love and Loyalty

What I Would Do

What i would do.
what i would do for a girl like you.
i would come when you call
i would make the bed if dirty
i would spend eternity in prison for you
i would offer you the first bite of our last bread
run 10 miles for water if you are thirsty
give you my jacket if you are cold
i would spend my last penny for your smile
give you my good beating heart for yours
i would do anything of your choice
i would give you my last dying breath to keep you warm and alive
i would always love you
no matter what.

My Little Girl

my little girl is
sweet and kind
has a love for God that's undenied
my little girl is full of excitement
she puts God before me
she dwindles on the thoughts of time
time to work
time to play
but my little girl has all the time for love
she doesn't run on batteries
she runs on the winds of youth
no matter what age she might be
there are no years to her
a spring of life comes from her
when you tell her you love her
her face brightens
her hair gets blonder
and her face cracks while a smile appears
and everything before now vanishes
all evil things done to her by others have dissipated away
and she becomes the 4-year-old bouncing in pleasure once again
only to look back at you
with the wide, bright deer eyes
only to reply with
a giant hug and a full-lipped kiss on your face
this is my little girl i love dearly
only God can take her from me now.

Point of View

point of view.
seeing only one item
a prized possession
worth more than life itself
interceded with love
compassion, forgiveness, and joy
these are all the things men would want
from a beautiful angel such as you
a tender heart that can be crushed by a misspoken word
repulsed at a cruel thought of others
shattered by unseen hate
though these are just a few of a multitude of ideals
of why i love you
as well as a generous hand to the unfortunate
what i wouldn't give to know you
to have your hand touch mine
in any way
for a man to be held by you is a blessing
a godsend are you
to love the unlovable
to walk in your presence
to be shadowed by you
is a feeling that only a few can say they have had
it may not mean much from a wretch as i
I'd hope it would be worth a mustard seed

if it came from a man
who truly adores you as i speak my last i love you
while my lungs take their last breath
and hold your hand in a clutch
that you know i meant every sorry and i love you
through these last 47 years of marriage
let me go on that day
and only on that day our Lord has called for me
but not until that day
until then you will be my point of view

Awaiting

you come from nowhere
and yet you're closer than i have ever imagined
a broken soul watches your mind
listens to your angelic voice
a twinkle in your eyes
a smile in your heart
knowledge unseen
i hear the distress in you
timeless walks to the tavern
to fill a void that can only be filled by one
a softhearted woman you are
don't let the wolves find you
they are out there in packs
droning aimlessly to find their prey
a gentle woman child are you
kind, sweet, and honest
you have lived your life
in the sun
don't fall in the shadows, my dear

time conquers what's in its path
unknowing when it will arrive
there are friends that seek you
that will take you in
and care for you
that will love you back
be the hunter, not the hunted
you are strong
mended by will
watched over by God
walk with me, dear, we can see the sunsets at dusk
and the sunrise in the mornings
listen to the morning doves' cue at noon
take my hand in friendship
hold it firmly, it won't let you go
it is genuine, honest, and loyal
With time you will see

Dream a Little Dream

❖

dream a little dream.
in all the ways i know you
and all that i don't
i forever ask the Lord to know and keep you
in spirit, mind, and soul
you are the best thing i have ever been given
even my life is not worth to me what you are
the little noises you make as you sleep
your looks of surprise
the grunts of displeasure of me
the guttural moans of disbelief as a shock in horror
to be with you is a dream and a wish i have had for eternity
well, as long as my eternity has been
for you, baby girl, i want it all
to be with you one horrible day beats any other best day i have ever
had without you
and you wonder why i still wish upon stars and wish times?
not for another you
because there is none
but for us to have a better tomorrow.
so ye keep wishing those little wishes that i do

Scorpions Sunset

scorpions sunset
they said it would never happen
an epic challenge of 2 different entities
one was fire that couldn't be tamed
and the other life that is persistent in growing throughout time
heat of a soul that cannot be extinguished
by no chains, no cells, no bars, no teacher
a spreading flame devouring what was in its path
no concern about what was to be
to devour that which was weak,
to become a firestarter itself,
until it had reached one that was a power in itself
life....
a twitch from life as it looked into fire's path
a thought of why?
why destroy things so beautiful as you do?
passing a quivering breeze into the flame
fire responds—
you, my precious, will be burned by the flame
i warn you, my little unburned life
Don't get too close, I won't let you.

a 6-month journey to find the life
endures flame
a sickening thought the fire has
i will not be burned for i am the flame
nor will i be put out
i have met others like you, my dear life
walk with me
says life
i know it will hurt at times
for you are a destroyer of lives
you trust no one to be an inferno with you
i will not fear your fire
i am life, proud and full
i will tempt you
and you will trust in me when no one would
i will and can extinguish the fire in your soul
with an instant
a smile crosses over fire's lips
no!
this cannot be happening to fire
a sweet, tender kiss from life
pssssss
fire is a low simmer of coals
and they said it would never happen.

Through the Night

through the night
upon waking. you're not there. oh, how it felt as if you were.
your smell is on each and every pillow i touch.
longing for your comfort. i get none.
but knowing soon you will arrive.
sends deep chills across my smile
as i think how lovely it would be to see and hold you again.
knowing i could lose you at any moment.
drips a cold bead of sweat down my spine.
to know it is evident. i ask God to wait
until the passing of two moons in our night sky.
knowing it is not elementally possible for this.
i fear to look into the abyss of the cold black beyond.
i see no moon, no stars. a relief.
to know i have the most precious thing in life as love itself.
from a woman like you.
who has everything i could ever need and want from a woman.
a lover, a friend, a conscience when i am not.
i thank the heavens time and again.

there is nothing i could ask or want more than you fully.
just to be able to kiss your soft, moist lips. brings me to a world i have never known before.
a world of safety, belonging, and a time and space where i can be who i am and want to be.
i am an old broken soul. between worlds i live in with you.
a time lost before i met you. ages ago.
a clenching to strings that had broken each and every time.
until you passed me the rope to pull myself into your domain.
with a synch knot i hold on to you.
twirling on top of your knot with you.
we careen the worlds and galaxies beyond.
with one and only one demand of you. don't let go.
i am happy with you in the tangled web of love you have spun for me.

By the Moonlight

weary I was daydreaming on the shoreline,
thinking of times past, time wasted,
things should have been done,
money been spent,
lost opportunities,
thinking of a drink to settle the nerves,
a cold breeze blows by,
a winter warning of cold nights alone,
a fast hello,
echoes from the distance,
turn to look,
no one there,
"behind you, silly,"
surprised by you,
wind in your hair,
a grin on your face,
puzzled by why me?
come closer and talk,
frightened by the nervousness,
try to keep your cool, I think,
sit still, I won't bite, I promise, you laugh,
a wonderful sound of you to listen to,
so young,
childlike,
innocent,
pure,
sure,

angelic,

thoughts of,

why,

what do you want of me,

are you like them, too?

hours of no other false recollections, horror tales,

just fun, honest whispers in the night only the ocean can hear,

seeing the shivers run down your spine,

would you like my parka?

the first touch of your hand and I pass you my coat,

warm,

lovely,

as a spark passes through you,

you shutter as we touch fingers,

I'm sorry,

you say,

for what?

for making you jump, too,

you smile,

I know I did,

hehe,

I'm not used to being in company of something so beautiful as you,

your smile becomes a full, true smile,

a few moments go by,

speechless,

an owl calls in the night to its mate,

the breeze comes slower but warmer,

the moon is full in the night sky,
waves drift into shore as peaceful as the morning snow
drifts into the water,
your hand grasps mine,
follow me, I have something to show you,
unsure, I follow,
leaving fresh tracks of snow,
walking side by side,
from the oceanfront to the hills above,
a twinkle in your eyes,
you look at me,
we're here,
where?
home,
home?
yes, kiddo, home,
you see, from the beginning we met years ago,
you did not know me then,
of course I just met you,
but dear, that was 49 years ago,
I know,

but this is the end of our journey here,
you mean we died?
no,
not at all,
what, then?
here's where we begin, my love,

begin what?
eternity, darling,
see, past the clouds of time and space there was nothing,
and yet you were created for me,
you just didn't know this,
well???
just as I was created for you,
how do you know?
look at how when we hold each other,
how our lips bind together,
how you have the same things just opposite of me,
so the bindings of our hands tell it all,
no,
the way we connect is,
even how you think you're fatherless.
but there's one that
looms in the clouds
that walks beside us
listens to our every need
comforts us when we're
alone.
Look above. He is there
waiting for us to call on
Him.
We have never been alone
…and never will be.

In Splendor

I see you as gorgeous as you are.
With a smile like you just won a million.
And a glimmering eye as you stare deep into me.
Presenting you a gift of love from my soul.
Hair tied up in a bow.
Beautiful is the night sky.
Looking across a small lake is tranquility we possess.
A moon about to rise in its orange and red outlines.
Your face is bright and your eyes are as big as they can be.
In your evening dress.
Long as your hair.
Golden as the ring i have given you the year before.
Lovely are your thank-yous.
When i bend to kiss you and to run my hand by your lips.
As it is to say don't talk now.
To put my hands upon you to remind me that you are real.
And to know the beauty you possess.

Is what i had fallen in love with.
A wonderful woman as you are.
One who bandages me when hurt.
Feeds me when hungry.
One who loves me through my faults.
One to clothe me when i can't.
Is what i long for.
Between thick and thin.
There is no room for a no with you.
When all i have ever known is a yes.
There is a heaven i live in with you.
Where there is no negatives, no mistakes within our love.
Our love is perfect as you are.
Keep your eyes bright and illuminating just as your soul shines endlessly in the night.

Seasons

A spring sparrow flutters to perch atop a branch rest.
Within the howling winds of the plains.
Tired and weary is the sparrow.
The nectar of the sweet honeysuckle
is nourishment to the hummingbird.
The warming air is the beginning sign of spring and
cottontail baby bunnies are a start of a new wonder this year.
As the snow is melting the first flowers creep out of the ground.
Sounds of other birds fill the skies to welcome the new year.
The spring fawns dance in amazement, their new and young.
To be free and wonder the forests to grow and
continue the cycle of life. To be beautiful and carefree.
Like you, my little one.
After the snow has receded into the ground,
we can spread our wings and fly into a calm, warm wind.
To glide the thermals.
Dive into the stratosphere,
following the sun to find a grazing ground.
It will be just us two in our little world of wonder and exploration.
In our lives.
There is no other pasture i want to graze upon.
Come with me, little one.
Let's get lost in the thicket, be found by the moon together.
Until the morning sun opens our eyes.
All to do it over again.

Royal Within

✦

You wear your best today.
As i will also.
You shine in splendor.
Bedazzled is your blonde hair.
As if it were golden strands of purity.
A bow in your hair makes it divine.
Long is your gown.
White as a midday cloud.
Gracious are you.
Tiptoeing to me.
You ask.
How do i look?
As beautiful as the day i met you,
I replied.
You couldn't look any more precious to me.
Come, the dinner will start soon.
We will make it if we hurry.
Yes, dear, we will.
I only have a few shillings
I know, my beloved.
We have an invite by the queen herself.
We do?
Yes, we do.
What does the queen want of us paupers?
Good company, i guess.

Did you bring a gift?

No, i can't afford one.

There is a wishing well we can toss one shilling in and hope for the best.

Yes, my fair lady, we will do that.

Here we are, my bride.

"You there,

The one with the golden hair and lace.

Come and sit with your dear husband at my side.

Your highness?

Do you mean me and my husband?

Yes, you two, come to me and sit.

I saw you put in your coins in the well.

Do you think the well will multiply them?

No, your highness.

Just wishful thinking, as we are tots with our heads in the clouds.

You both spent your coins and now, how are you to pay taxes to me?

Awe, have not a shilling left nor a dry piece of bread to eat.

My wife says that she has an invitation from you for a banquet?

Oh, she says so?

Yes, your highness.

Let me see it.

This is not an invitation for dinner, you ninny.

This is a lottery plate with the winners' names.

For being royalty as i, the queen.

I have the right to do with you as i will.
The lottery was one of two choices.
Do you pick the golden bag or do you pick the burlap bag?
A short while later they picked the burlap bag.
I choose the bag of burlap.
For that is what i wear.
A fine pick, commoner.
You open the bag.
And to our astonishment we find golden pieces.
Too many for your little hands to count.
Now if you had chosen the golden bag it would have shown me greed.
That would have exiled you from my land.
Now take your riches, my once paupers, and be away with you.
And don't forget, every Sunday i have a banquet for you ones that have a second chance in life as you do now.

Searchin

A morning breeze as you open your eyes.
Tells you good morning with the dew surrounding you.
A glint of sunshine dries you in the warm draft.
The osprey calls to its mate to say,
She's awake now in its soft warble.
As if they were protecting you as you slept.
The soft grass you lay in.
With a thought of the miles you tread the day before.
You are still achy looking for the one you rely on.
Streams, hills, and mountains you have seen.
Treacherous paths you have crossed.
The beating sun and the frigid nights you have wept.
But to no avail have you found what you were looking for.
Still it is unfound.
By the sun and moon do you travel.

The wind guides your path.
Into the thorns and soft grasses of life.
Still you tread on.
You grow tired.
Until.
You ask your inner self.
Why am i lost?
You hear from within.
A hunger pang and you realize.
It's not a place or food to keep on, that you need.
It's a thirst of knowledge you seek.
You look up and
You understand.
That it's a quest to grow within the presence of the one who created.
Everything you embarked upon

The Note

smelling the flowers by the path you're on.
you are in a daze by the sounds behind you.
as the cardinals sing of your presence.
you are a delight to the forest.
looking for your soul to be.
beautiful in all ways are you.
astonished by a branch that has a blue ribbon tied to it.
with a note.
a short letter.
you read this note.
(you will be found by the lover)
questioning.
who left this…
is it to me?
a little farther you walk.
another note you see on a bush of blue.
(safely you will return)
pondering?
who left these??
am I being fooled?
yet you see the brightest red lily…

you bend down to smell it,
and find a lost golden ring.
it is the most gorgeous band you have ever seen.
engraved on the band is your name.
shocked.
you are in dismay.
did I lose this before?
is this a trick?
you ask the sky.
lord.
my beloved god of mine…
I am scared.
I see these signs that point to me.
but what for?
show me, lord, i know not.
a last letter blows by you.
you pick it up…
and read this.
(I have walked by you within these miles,
I have knelt by you, bottled up your tears.)
(here, my lovely, you don't need to hold these any longer,
walk with me, by me, and you will never be lost nor scared,
trust in me, princess, you will find your way home to me…)
woosh, your notes vanish….

CPSIA information can be obtained
at www.ICGtesting.com
Printed in the USA
BVHW021457080421
604474BV00006B/86